Grandpa Takes Me to THE MOON

TIMOTHY R. GAFFNEY

PICTURES BY BARRY ROOT

TAMBOURINE BOOKS NEW YORK

To Jean, my wife —T.R.G.

For Sam —B.V.R.

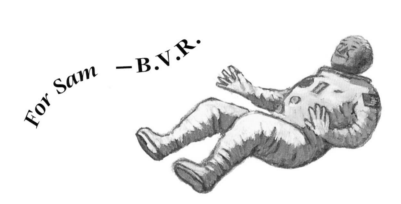

Text copyright © 1996 by Timothy R. Gaffney. Illustrations copyright © 1996 by Barrett V. Root.

All rights reserved. No part of this book may be reproduced or utilized in any form or by any means, electronic or mechanical, including photocopying, recording, or by any information storage or retrieval system, without permission in writing from the Publisher. Inquiries should be addressed to Tambourine Books, a division of William Morrow & Company, Inc., 1350 Avenue of the Americas, New York, New York 10019. Printed in the United States of America. Book design by Golda Laurens. The text type is Veljovic Book. The illustrations were painted in watercolor and gouache on paper. Library of Congress Cataloging in Publication Data: Gaffney, Timothy R. Grandpa takes me to the moon / by Timothy R. Gaffney ; illustrated by Barry Root.—1st ed. p. cm. Summary: A child whose grandfather was an astronaut always asks Grandpa for a bedtime story in which the two of them blast off for the moon together. [1. Space flight to the moon—Fiction. 2. Moon—Exploration—Fiction. 3. Astronauts—Fiction. 4. Grandfathers—Fiction.] I Root, Barry, ill. II. Title. PZ7.G1195Gr 1996 [E]—dc20 95-53748 CIP AC ISBN 0-688-13937-X (TR). —ISBN 0-688-13938-8 (LE)

3 5 7 9 10 8 6 4

First edition

HISTORICAL NOTE

Between December 1968 and December 1972, men from earth made nine voyages to the moon as part of America's Apollo program. The voyages included six lunar landings. Twelve men walked on the moon's surface; all returned safely. Their stories still excite us, but no one has tried to follow them. The technology to do it exists; all that is needed is the will.

The idea for this book resulted from a meeting several years ago at which I introduced my daughter Kim to James Irwin, an *Apollo 15* astronaut who walked on the moon in 1971. The meeting was small and informal, and he talked to her at length about his adventure. A few months later, Mr. Irwin died. It struck me how long it has been since these men made their journeys, and how quickly we are losing the opportunity to hear them tell their stories.

A long time ago, my grandpa went to the moon.
  My parents have told me about it a hundred times. But I like it best when he tells me. Whenever he visits, I ask him to tell me a bedtime story about his trip to the moon.

I get all tucked under my covers. Grandpa turns out the light to make the room dark. "Dark like space," he says. Sometimes the moon glows outside my window like a lamp in the night sky. As Grandpa tells his story, I close my eyes and imagine I'm going with him.

To get to the moon, we go to Florida first. That's where the rocket is. The sun is hot. A steady breeze blows off the ocean, and we can smell salt in the air.

The rocket stands like a skyscraper. It's taller than the Statue of Liberty. Most of it is engines and fuel. At the top is a tiny capsule. That's our spaceship. Another astronaut joins us. We ride an elevator up to the capsule.

Inside the capsule are three couches. Grandpa sits on the left.
The other astronaut sits on the right. I sit in the middle.

The rocket blasts off with a terrific roar. The sudden speed pushes us into our couches. The capsule shakes. The rocket falls away in stages.

Now we coast, and we don't feel any weight. We float, and so does anything that's loose.

It takes four days to reach the moon. We loop into an orbit and circle it, just like a little moon.

Grandpa and I float through the capsule's nose into another spaceship that will take us down to the moon. It's only big enough for two. "See you later," the other astronaut says.

We fire the moon lander's rocket. We slow down and drop toward the moon. We fire the rocket again to land.

We touch down on a flat plain with round, gray mountains on the horizon. There are no colors, just shades of gray. The sun is shining, but the sky is black like night. There is no air on the moon to make the sky blue. Space and black sky come right down to the ground.

We put on our space helmets. We have to back out the little door on our hands and knees. We climb down the ladder and step onto the moon.

The surface is soft and gray. There are no green trees or grass,
no brown rivers, no blue lakes, no white clouds. There are rocks
strewn about and craters that look like bowls in the ground.

The soil is dark and powdery. It's like a fine dust. There's no
wind to blow it around, so it covers everything. Our boots make
footprints in the dust.

Our spacesuits are thick and heavy, but everything weighs much less on the moon. Grandpa bounces when he walks. I pick up a rock and let it drop. It falls in slow motion to the ground. Dust splashes up around it and falls back like water.

We unload a buggy. Grandpa calls it the lunar rover. We drive
away on it until the moon lander looks like a little toy.

We stop several times to scoop up soil and rocks to take back to earth. Pieces of the moon. We scoop them up and put them in bags, just like that.

High overhead is the earth. It reminds me of the moon when it's almost full, but its bright side is colored blue and white by oceans and clouds.

"Time to go home," Grandpa says.

Before we leave, we plant an American flag on the moon. A small arm on the flagpole holds the flag out like it's waving in a breeze. We step back and salute it. Then we climb back into the moon lander and blast off.

We return to the capsule, and it takes us back to earth. Splash! We're home.

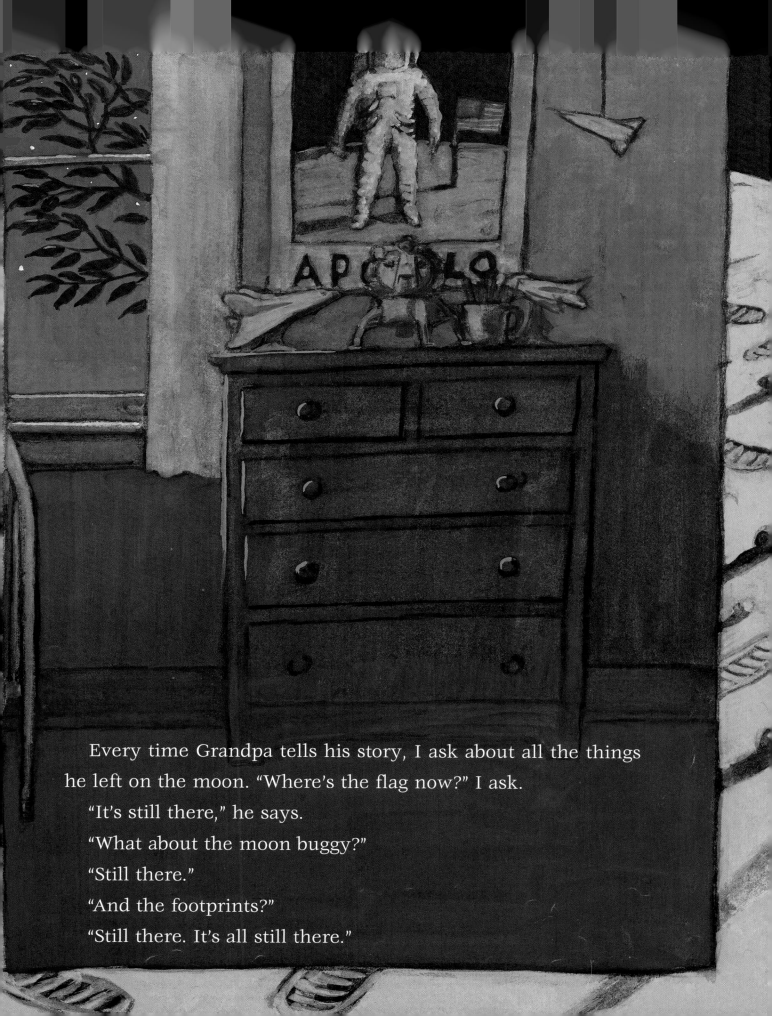

Every time Grandpa tells his story, I ask about all the things
he left on the moon. "Where's the flag now?" I ask.

"It's still there," he says.

"What about the moon buggy?"

"Still there."

"And the footprints?"

"Still there. It's all still there."

Then I ask, "Grandpa, can I ever go to the moon?"

He smiles and says, "Why sure, if you like. Then you'll have the story to tell your grandchildren."